ENZO
AND THE FOURTH OF JULY RACES

Garth Stein
Illustrated by R. W. Alley

HARPER
An Imprint of HarperCollinsPublishers

For Tyrone, a big dog with a gentle soul
—G.S.

To Barbara and Manny and J. M. Fields,
with love and "noglaxia"!
—R.W.A. and Z.B.A.

Enzo and the Fourth of July Races   Text copyright © 2017 by Garth Stein   Additional text edits by Zoë B. Alley and R. W. Alley   Illustrations copyright © 2017 by R. W. Alley   All rights reserved. Manufactured in China.   No part of this book may be used or reproduced in any manner whatsoever without written permission except in the case of brief quotations embodied in critical articles and reviews. For information address HarperCollins Children's Books, a division of HarperCollins Publishers, 195 Broadway, New York, NY 10007.   www.harpercollinschildrens.com   ISBN 978-0-06-238059-3   The artist used pen and ink, pencil, watercolor, gouache, acrylics, and coffee spills on paper to create the illustrations for this book.   Typography by Rachel Zegar   17 18 19 20 21   SCP   10 9 8 7 6 5 4 3 2 1   ❖   First Edition

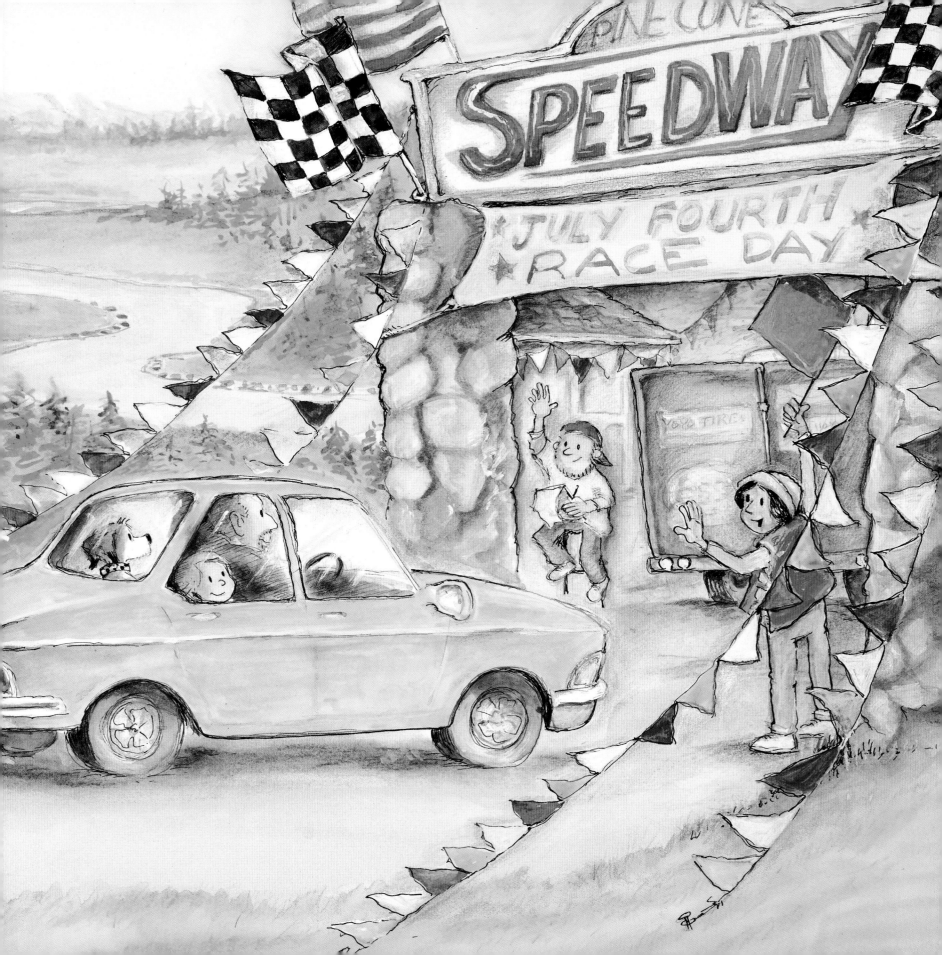

It's nearly the Fourth of July, which means it's time for the big race weekend. I love it when we go to the races on Independence Day because there are so many people, and everybody is happy to see each other. And this year, Zoë is big enough to race on her own in the Kids' Kart Challenge!

It's a big race for Denny in the season points championship, but it's a *bigger* race for Zoë, who will be in her first race against other kids.

"What if I'm not fast enough?" Zoë whispers into my ear.

She's very fast, so I'm not concerned. She's been driving karts since she was nearly my size. But I can tell she isn't feeling confident, so I stay with her instead of following my instinct to chase the crows that are looking to steal food. (I have never trusted a crow.)

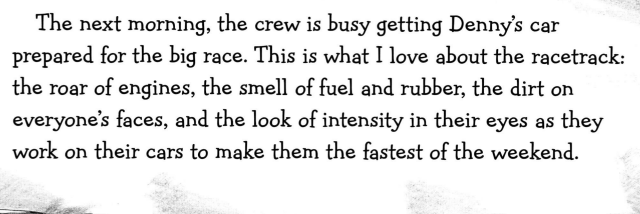

The next morning, the crew is busy getting Denny's car prepared for the big race. This is what I love about the racetrack: the roar of engines, the smell of fuel and rubber, the dirt on everyone's faces, and the look of intensity in their eyes as they work on their cars to make them the fastest of the weekend.

And I also like that sometimes someone drops a hot dog and doesn't notice.

While Denny's car is being prepped, he takes
Zoë to register for the Kids' Kart Challenge.

When the practice session is over, one of the fastest kids looks at the registration clipboard.

"Let's see who's going to get second place," he says boastfully. "Hey! A *girl* signed up for the race! Girls aren't fast drivers. I guess she'll be our back marker!"

I growl softly at the kid, but he doesn't hear me because he's the kind of person who can only hear his own words.

"Let it go, Enzo," Denny says to me. "We'll do our talking on the track."

I let it go, because Denny is much wiser than me, and I trust his judgment. But I really want to bite that kid on his back marker.

As we leave the kart track, Zoë breaks away and runs back to registration. She scratches her name off the entry list. When she rejoins us, Denny kneels down and puts his hand on her shoulder.

"A wise man once told me," he says to her, "'There is no dishonor in losing the race. There is only dishonor in not racing because you are afraid to lose.'"

Zoë doesn't reply. I wonder if she's afraid. I hadn't thought so; she's very fast. But maybe it's something I don't understand because I am a dog.

"I just don't want to," she says finally.

I can hear in her voice that what she really wants
to do is cry.

"Okay, then," Denny says after a moment. "I respect
your decision, and I love you whether or not you race.
Okay?"

"Okay, Daddy."

It's time for Denny's practice session. Denny's crew chief, Johnny Mac, and Zoë and I go to the stands to watch. We're all wearing radio headsets to protect our ears, but also so we can hear Denny call in to Johnny Mac about how his car is driving.

As Denny's car races around the track, we can see that he's not as fast as the other cars.

"How's the car, Denny?" Johnny Mac says into his microphone. "You're way off pace."

"Something with the setup," we hear Denny's voice crackle through the headsets. "She's loose. Real loose. And she's pushing through turn nine."

"Okay, bring her in," Johnny Mac says, shaking his head.

"I'm not sure it's the car that needs fixing," he tells us.

"I wish Zoë would get out there and give it a shot," Denny says to Johnny Mac. "Even if she doesn't do well."

"If *that's* what you're thinking about on the track, then don't race," Johnny Mac says. "If your head's not in the right place, you're putting yourself and other drivers in danger."

"You're right," Denny says. "Maybe I should sit this one out. I'm distracted."

Johnny Mac nods, but he doesn't seem happy.

"Why did you change your mind about racing?" Johnny Mac asks Zoë.

"A boy said girls aren't fast," Zoë answers sheepishly.

"What a lug nut!" Johnny Mac cries. "There are some awesome girl racers out there who could teach that kid a thing or two about speed!"

It's true! Shirley Muldowney, Lyn St. James, Janet Guthrie, and Danica Patrick . . . to name a few I have had the privilege of watching on television!

"I know how fast you are," Johnny Mac tells her. "Your dad knows. Heck, even *Enzo* knows—"

I bark twice!

"See?" he says. "But none of us matter, Zoë, because none of us are *you*. You have to believe in *yourself!*"

Denny doesn't look like he's listening, but I can tell he is. I nudge Zoë with my muzzle, and she pats my head. Then she looks up at Johnny Mac, determined.

"I believe in me, Johnny Mac," she says.

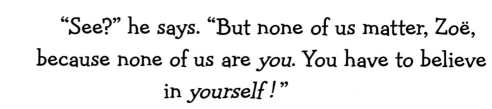

"Then go get some practice," Johnny Mac says. "And put your name back on that entry list so I can get your father to believe in *himself*, too. Because *I* believe you both can win your races this weekend."

Zoë's kart zips this way and that and around the turns. Round and round, she flies by so quickly that the bored teenagers take notice.

Around and around, until we are all grinning. She pulls into the pits and climbs out of the kart.

"You're up there with the best of them," one of the teenagers says. "You should definitely race."

Zoë nods and puts her name back on the entry list.

I see Denny watching us. I know he's proud of her, too.

Qualifying for the races is very tense for me, because both Denny and Zoë are qualifying at the same time.

I have to run back and forth to make sure they're both driving well.
They don't realize how much work it is for me to look after them!

But maybe neither of them did *so* well. They both qualify midpack. Maybe I didn't help them after all.

I'm worried about Zoë because she hasn't yet learned how much she has to believe in herself to become a champion.

"Not bad . . . for a girl," the fast kid boasts. "But you'll never catch me."

"I'll do my talking on the track," Zoë says.

Which I think is a good answer.

After the racing is finished for the day, we go out onto the track. When we reach turn two, Denny gets down on his knees and feels the pavement with his hands. He studies the turn from every angle.

"Did you lose something?" a corner worker asks as he rolls up his flags.

"I lost about a half second," Denny says. "And I'm pretty sure I lost it right here, in this turn."

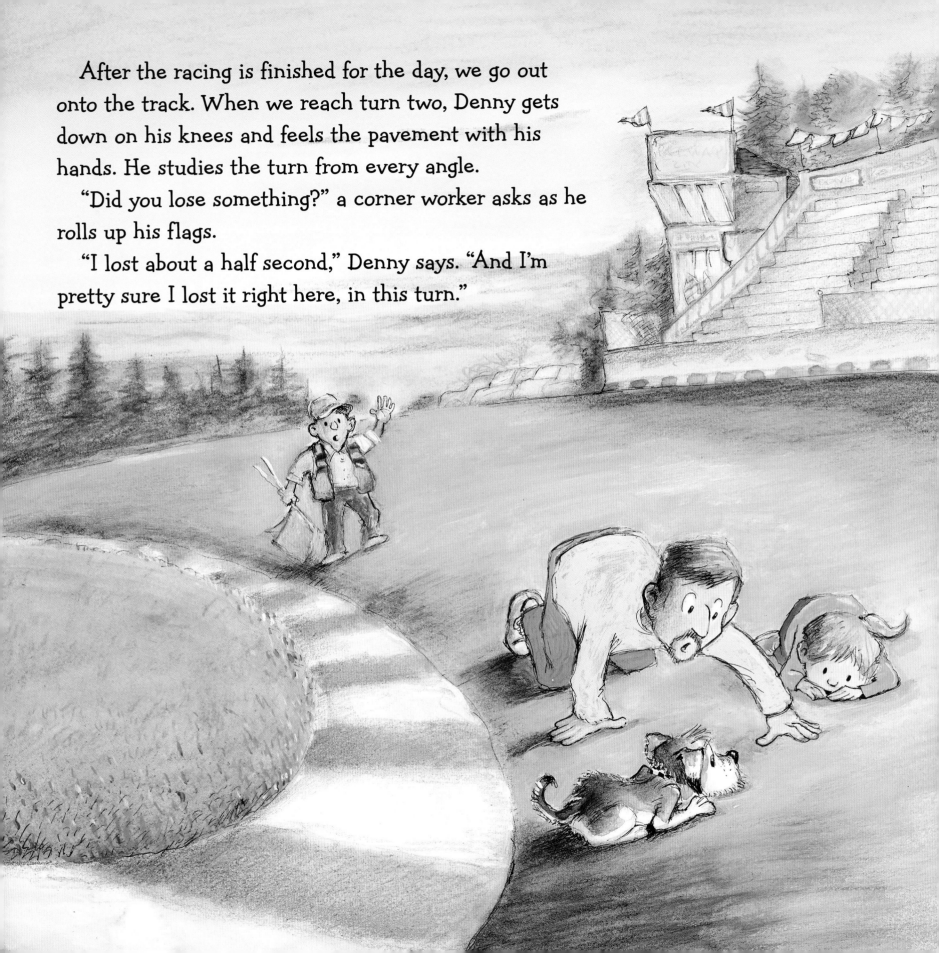

"You know," the corner worker says, "the fast guys brake a little earlier here, and they get on the throttle sooner. The more speed you have here, the more you'll carry over there."

"What do you think, Zoë?" Denny asks. "Does that look like a half second to you?"

Zoë scratches her chin and squints at the tarmac. She looks like her dad.

"Just about a half second," she says.

"I think so, too."

Everyone has stopped working . . . except Denny and Zoë. They crawl around the kart track looking for half seconds. I love Zoë and Denny, but this is too much work for me. I've been running around all day in the hot sun, watching them qualify! I doze by our neighbor's fire, which is much easier than searching for half seconds.

It's finally time.

Denny's race begins first. It takes
him a few laps to learn the new way
through turn two, but when he gets it down, he
works his way to the front of the pack and leads
the second half of the race. He pulls away from the
pack of cars behind him and takes the checkered
flag without a worry. He waves to the crowd in
victory as he takes his cooldown lap.

Zoë's race is next and is much tougher. It's hard for
her to get past the other karts, but she and Denny must
have found that half second on the kart track last night.
Soon she's neck and neck with the fast kid. The two of
them leave all the other karts in their dust.

Try as she might, Zoë can't get past the fast kid. It's almost the last lap as they come into a sweeping turn, and Zoë appears to lift off the throttle. Her kart slows, and the fast kid dives into the turn. I don't understand why she's letting him get away. But then she jumps on the throttle early, swoops inside, and easily zips past his kart.

Oh, the fast kid is not happy, and he bangs his steering wheel. Zoë knows he's not thinking about racing anymore; he's worried about losing, and that's all she needs.

Zoë wins by nearly half a lap. Everybody in the crowd cheers! I bark twice!

Zoë looks good on the top step of the podium. She's full of smiles, but Denny and Johnny Mac are smiling even more.

"I guess you kicked my butt," the fast kid says to Zoë after the award ceremony.

"Well," Zoë says with a laugh, "your butt's pretty big, so it wasn't hard to kick."

"Yeah, I shouldn't have said that about girls not being fast. Sorry."

Zoë accepts his apology with great dignity.

"But how did you do that in turn eight?" he asks. "You were behind me and then, suddenly, you were driving away! That's some trick!"

"My dad and a corner worker helped me find a half second last night," Zoë says. "Want me to show you?"

"Yeah!"

Here's what I love about the Fourth of July races: I love seeing old friends, making new friends, and spending time with my family. I love learning secrets from corner workers and learning how to believe in myself. I love the hot sun, and the smoldering campfires, and the dropped hot dogs. But most of all, I love watching the fireworks at the end of race night with Denny and Zoë, who are my favorite people of all.

GLOSSARY

Back Marker—The slowest car in the race. When he or she is lapped, the front-runners think, "There's our back marker."

Checkered Flag—The most important of flags, the black and white "checker" means you have won the race! It is also used to end practice and qualifying sessions.

Cooldown Lap—After the checkered flag ends the race or practice session, drivers take one more lap to cool off their brakes and tires before returning to the paddock.

Corner Worker—Wonderful people who watch each corner of a racetrack to signal to race participants with different colored flags used to keep the track safe. They also stand ready to rescue a driver who might be in trouble due to an incident on the track. Drivers always salute the corner workers on their cooldown lap.

Jack Stands—Heavy metal devices used to hold the car above the ground so crew members can easily work on the car.

Lift—When a driver takes his or her foot off the gas pedal in order to slow the car, without affecting the balance as braking would, it is called "lifting."

Loose—A car that has a tendency to spin when going into a turn "too hot," or with too much speed, is called "loose."

Lug Nut—A small but heavy metal nut used to hold the wheel to the hub so the wheel doesn't fall off. (Lug nuts aren't very smart.)

Midpack—The "pack" refers to the group of race cars in a certain class or race. Front-runners, midpack, and back markers are terms used to define where a given racer stands.

Pace—Set by the front-runner, the pace is what every racer wants to keep up with. If you're "off pace," you are falling behind. If you're "setting the pace," you're leading the race.

Paddock—An area next to the race track where racing teams assemble to work on their cars.

Pushing—The opposite of being "loose," a car that "pushes" doesn't turn in when it's supposed to and wants to go in a straight line.

Qualifying Session—Racers participate in a qualifying session to set their best lap time, sometimes called a "hot lap." Drivers are then placed on the starting grid based on their qualifying time, the fastest being in first, or "pole position," and the slowest being the back marker.

Season Points Championship—There are many races in a season, and each race awards points to the top finishers. The racer who accumulates the most points by the end of the season is called the Season Points Champion.

Setup—Racetracks are different, as are weather conditions. A car has many adjustments that can be made to work best with these different conditions. The adjustments used for a particular session are called the setup.

Tarmac—What racers call the road surface of the racetrack.

Throttle—The device that controls the flow of fuel to the engine, controlled by the rightmost pedal of a car or kart, otherwise known as the "gas pedal."